MONSTER BLOOD IV

Look for more Goosebumps books
by R.L. Stine:
(see back of book for a complete listing)

MONSTER BLOOD IV

R.L. STINE

AN
APPLE
PAPERBACK

SCHOLASTIC INC.
New York Toronto London Auckland Sydney
New Delhi Hong Kong

ISBN-13: 978-0-590-39987-6

This edition is for sale in the Indian subcontinent only.

First Scholastic printing, December 1993
Reprinted by Scholastic India Pvt. Ltd.,
June, July, August 2007; January, March, September 2008;
January, August 2010; May 2011; January 2012;
July, October 2013; July, August, December 2014
June, October 2015; January; May 2017

Printed at JJ Offset Printers, Noida

Evan Ross was thinking about Monster Blood. He thought about Monster Blood a lot.

Evan wished he had never discovered Monster Blood. The sticky, slimy green goo had to be the most dangerous substance on Earth.

Evan knew that as soon as you open a can of Monster Blood, you are *doomed*. The Monster Blood will grow and grow — and suck up everything in its path.

And if you accidentally eat some of the green goo — *look out!* A tiny chunk of Monster Blood had turned Cuddles, the classroom hamster, into a growling monster as big as a gorilla!

And when Evan accidentally swallowed a little bit of it, he shot up taller than his house. It was not the happiest day of Evan's life. It was a day he kept trying to forget.

So why was he thinking about Monster Blood today?

His green sweater reminded him of Monster Blood. He had begged his mom not to make the sweater green. But she had already started knitting it. Too late to change colors.

"You look good in green," she told him. "It brings out your eyes."

"I don't want to bring out my eyes," Evan told her.

He wanted to scream. The yarn she used was greener than the Jolly Green Giant! He pictured himself trapped inside a giant green blob of Monster Blood.

"Wear it to your cousin Kermit's," Mrs. Ross instructed him.

"I don't need a sweater," he protested. "Just put it in my suitcase."

"Wear it. It's winter," she insisted. "It gets cold, even here in Atlanta."

"I don't want to stay at Kermit's," Evan grumbled, pulling the sweater over his head. Yuck. Green — and *itchy*. "How long are you and Dad going to be out West?"

"Only nine or ten days," his mother replied.

"*Only?*" Evan cried, struggling into the tight wool sleeves. "I'll die! Aunt Dee's food is so horrible! She puts that hot sauce on everything. Even brownies!"

"Your aunt does *not* put hot sauce on brownies," Mrs. Ross replied sternly. "She likes to make spicy food, but —"

"I'll explode!" Evan insisted. "And that geeky little creep, Kermit —"

"Don't call your cousin a geeky little creep," Mrs. Ross scolded.

"Well, he *is* one — isn't he?" Evan demanded.

"That's beside the point," his mom said. She pulled the green sweater down over Evan's waist and admired it. "It fits perfectly. And I like that shade of green."

"I look like a ripe watermelon," Evan grumbled.

"Don't forget, Aunt Dee is paying you to baby-sit Kermit," his mom reminded him. She handed him his suitcase. "You want to go to sleepaway camp this summer, right? Well, you can't go to camp unless you earn the money to pay for it."

"I know, I know." He kissed his mom good-bye.

"Your dad and I will call you when we get to Tucson," Mrs. Ross said. "Take good care of Kermit. And don't give Aunt Dee a hard time."

"I won't eat till you get back," Evan told her. "I'll probably weigh ten pounds."

His mom laughed.

She thinks I'm joking, Evan thought bitterly.

He hoisted up his backpack and his suitcase and headed for the back door. He passed a mirror in the hall and caught a glimpse of himself in the sweater. "Sick," he muttered. "I look like a pickle."

"Evan — what did you say?" his mom called.

"I said, 'Thanks for the cool sweater!'" he called back to her.

A few seconds later, he was walking through backyards, making his way to Kermit's house at the end of the block. Maybe I can hide this sweater somewhere, he thought. Maybe I can give it to Kermit as a Christmas present.

No. Kermit is such a shrimp, the sweater would be down to his knees.

It was a sunny, crisp winter day. The sweater glowed under the bright sunlight. It really did remind Evan of Monster Blood.

He pictured the slimy green gunk. He pictured heaps and heaps of it, oozing over the backyards he passed, bubbling and pulsing.

As he walked along, Evan had no idea that he was about to have another Monster Blood adventure.

He had no idea that he was about to discover a whole new kind of Monster Blood.

He had no idea that the green Monster Blood was silly kid stuff compared to the Monster Blood he was about to find.

2

He was nearly to Kermit's backyard, still thinking about Monster Blood, when a dark shadow swept over him.

He raised his eyes. "Conan —!" he gasped.

A big hulk of a boy loomed in front of him, hands clenched into big fists, blocking Evan's path. He lived in the house behind Kermit's.

His name was Conan Barber. But everyone called him Conan the Barbarian. That's because he was the biggest, meanest kid in Atlanta.

Conan placed the heel of his size-twelve sneaker on top of Evan's shoe and stomped down hard.

Evan yelped in pain. "Conan — why'd you do that?" he squealed.

"Do what?" Conan grunted. He narrowed his cold blue eyes at Evan.

"You — you crushed my foot!" Evan gasped.

"Accidents happen," Conan replied. He snickered. Despite the winter cold, he wore a gray muscle shirt and tight black spandex bike shorts. "Here. Let me fix it," he offered.

And he stomped down with all his might on Evan's other shoe.

"Owwwwwww." Evan took a few painful hops, holding his throbbing foot. "What's the big idea?"

"Breaking in my new sneakers," Conan replied, snickering again.

Evan wanted to wipe the smile off Conan's face. But how do you wipe the smile off a kid who's built like a *Monster Truck*?

"I've got to go," Evan said quietly. He picked up his suitcase and motioned with his head toward Kermit's house.

"Hey —!" Conan stared down at the ground. Then he raised his eyes to Evan. "Not so fast. You got the bottoms of my sneakers dirty."

"Excuse me?" Evan tried to step around Conan. But Conan blocked his path.

"Brand-new sneakers," Conan grumbled. "And you got the bottoms dirty."

"But — but —" Evan sputtered.

"Oh, well." Conan sighed. "I'll let you go this time."

Evan's heart pounded. He breathed a loud sigh of relief. "You will? You'll let me go?"

Conan nodded. He swept a beefy hand back through his wavy blond hair. "Yeah. You caught me in a good mood. Get going."

"Th-thanks," Evan stammered.

Conan stepped aside. Evan started past him.

He stopped when he heard a high, shrill voice ring out: "Leave my cousin alone!"

"Oh, noooo," Evan moaned. He turned to see Kermit running across the grass.

"Leave Evan alone!" Kermit called. He waved a tiny fist at Conan. "Pick on somebody your own size!"

"Kermit — stay out of this!" Evan shouted.

Kermit stepped up beside Evan. He was tiny and skinny. He had a pile of white-blond hair, a serious face, and round black eyes behind red plastic-framed glasses.

Standing next to Conan, he reminded Evan of a little ant. A bug that Conan could easily crush with one tromp of his heavy-duty size twelves.

"Take a walk, Conan!" Kermit squeaked. "Give Evan a break!"

Conan's eyes narrowed to angry slits. "I *was* going to give Evan a break," he growled. "Until you came along. But now I guess I have to teach you both a lesson."

He turned and grabbed the front of Evan's sweater.

3

"Evan — what happened to your sweater?" Aunt Dee demanded.

Evan set his suitcase down on the kitchen floor. "Well ..."

The left sleeve of his new sweater was normal length. Conan had taken the right sleeve and pulled it ... pulled ... pulled ... until the sleeve dragged on the ground.

"Mom made one sleeve a little too.long," Evan explained. He didn't want to tell his aunt about Conan.

Why look for trouble?

Conan promised that next time he'd pull Evan's right arm until it fit the sleeve!

"Evan picked a fight with Conan," Kermit reported.

Aunt Dee's mouth dropped open. "You shouldn't start fights, Evan."

Evan glared at Kermit. Why was the little creep always trying to get Evan in trouble?

"That boy Conan is big," Aunt Dee commented. "You really shouldn't pick on him."

Good advice, Evan thought bitterly. He lifted the mile-long sweater sleeve, then let it drop back to the floor.

"I'm going to fix Conan," Kermit declared. "I mixed up a formula that grows hair. I'm going to give it to Conan to drink — and he'll grow hair on his tongue. Whenever he tries to talk, he'll just go, 'Woffff woffff.' "

Aunt Dee laughed. "Kermit, stop!" she scolded. "You're starting to sound like a mad scientist!"

"I *am* a mad scientist!" Kermit declared proudly.

He and his mother laughed. But Evan couldn't even force a smile.

It's no joke, Evan thought. Kermit really *is* a mad scientist. He spends all his time down in his lab in the basement mixing bottles of green stuff with bottles of blue stuff.

One afternoon down in the lab, Evan asked Kermit what he was trying to discover. "I'm searching for a secret formula," Kermit replied, pouring a red liquid into a test tube.

"A secret formula that will do what?" Evan had asked.

"How should I know?" Kermit exclaimed. "It's secret!"

Now Evan had to spend the next ten days watching Kermit do his mad scientist act. And somehow he had to keep Kermit out of trouble.

9

"I'm so glad you're staying with us," Aunt Dee told Evan. "I just think it's great that you two cousins are so close."

"Yeah. Great," Evan muttered.

"Wofff wofff!" Kermit declared, giggling.

Aunt Dee led the two of them to Kermit's room at the back of the house. Kermit had a foldout bed where Evan would sleep.

Books and computer disks and papers and science magazines cluttered the floor. Evan had to step around a giant plastic model of the solar system to get to the dresser.

Aunt Dee helped him unpack his suitcase. Then she said, "You two run along. Go outside or something. I'm going into the kitchen to make dinner."

Dinner. The word sent a chill down Evan's back.

"What are we having?" he asked.

"It's a surprise," Aunt Dee told him.

Another chill.

"I brought my Super-Soaker," Evan told Kermit. "Let's go outside and have a water fight."

Kermit shook his head. "I don't think so." He led the way down the basement stairs to his science lab. "I want to show you something."

Evan stared at the shelves of jars and bottles and test tubes, all brimming with mysterious, dangerous materials. "I really don't feel safe —" he started.

Something bumped him hard from behind.

Evan spun around and gazed down at Dogface, Kermit's huge sheepdog. "Stop bumping me!" Evan snapped.

The dog stuck out his fat tongue and licked Evan's hand. It left a sticky gob of dog drool in his palm.

"Dogface likes you," Kermit said.

"Yuck," Evan groaned. He searched the lab table for a paper towel to wipe off the gunk.

"I want to try a little test," Kermit told him.

"No way!" Evan protested. "No little tests! The last time you tried a little test, you turned my nose blue."

"That was a mistake," Kermit replied. "This test is different. This test isn't dangerous." He raised his right hand. "I swear."

"What do I have to do?" Evan asked warily. "Drink something and have my tongue grow hair?"

Kermit shook his head. "No. I'm not ready to test that on a human yet."

"Good," Evan said, relieved. "Let's get our Super-Soakers and go outside." Evan really wanted to have a water fight. It was the only time he was allowed to attack Kermit and get away with it!

"After the test," Kermit replied. "The test only takes a minute. I promise."

Evan sighed. "Okay. What do I have to do?"

Kermit held up a black bandanna. "A blindfold," he said. "Put it on."

"Excuse me?" Evan cried, backing away. "Do you really think I'm going to let you blindfold me?"

"It isn't dangerous!" Kermit insisted in his high, shrill voice. "I just want to see if you can identify something. That's all. It will take a second."

Evan argued with his cousin for a while longer. But he ended up slipping on the blindfold. "Promise we'll go outside after this?"

"Promise," Kermit replied. He checked to make sure Evan's blindfold was tight. Then he took Evan's hand and lifted it to a big glass jar.

He pushed Evan's hand into the jar. "Tell me what's in the jar," Kermit instructed.

Staring at total blackness, Evan wrapped his hand around something warm and prickly.

"Hmmmm . . ." What is it? he wondered. What could it be?

As he tried to identify it, he felt something crawl up the back of his hand. It slipped under his shirt cuff and crawled up his arm.

"Huh?"

He felt a soft, pinching sensation on his hand.

Something prickled his wrist.

What is it? What *is* it?

He couldn't take it anymore. He ripped away the blindfold.

Gazed into the jar.

And then let out a horrified scream.

4

"Tarantulas?" Evan shrieked.

One of the hairy creatures clung to his arm underneath his shirtsleeve. Another inched its way across the back of his hand.

"Don't scream like that," Kermit warned, his eyes locked on Evan's arm.

"What kind of test is this?" Evan shrieked. "What are you trying to prove?"

Kermit didn't look up from the crawling tarantulas. "Someone told me that tarantulas won't bite you," he explained. "Unless they sense your fear."

"Are you *kidding* me?" Evan cried. "Sense my *fear*?"

"Ssshhhh." Kermit raised a finger to his lips. "Be very calm. Calm . . . calm . . ." He grinned at Evan. "This is an interesting experiment — isn't it?"

"I'll kill you!" Evan screamed. "I'll *kill* you for this, Kermit! When I'm finished with you, you'll go 'woffff woffff' for the rest of your life!"

"Careful," Kermit warned softly. "Your arm is shaking. Don't let them see your fear."

Evan struggled to steady his arm. One tarantula prickled his wrist. Another one stood on the back of his hand.

"Get these *off*!" Evan demanded in a frantic whisper. "I'm warning you — HEEEEY!"

Evan felt a hard bump from behind.

Dogface again!

Startled, Evan's hands shot up — and two tarantulas went flying.

One landed with a soft *THUD* on the lab table.

The other landed on Evan's head.

Evan gasped. He felt eight pointy tarantula legs scrambling through his hair.

"Don't upset it," Kermit instructed. "Be very calm. Don't let it know you're afraid. A tarantula bite can be very painful."

"Hey, guys — what's going on down there?" Aunt Dee's voice rang through the basement.

"Evan is playing with my tarantulas," Kermit reported.

Playing?

Evan wanted to scream. He pictured Kermit eating a tarantula sandwich.

No. That's not a good enough punishment, he decided.

"Well, it's too nice a day to stay down in the basement playing with spiders," Aunt Dee scolded.

"My tarantulas aren't just any old spiders!" Kermit fumed.

"Evan, your friend Andy is here," Aunt Dee called down. "I think all three of you should go outside and get some fresh air."

"Andy?" Evan called. Without thinking, he started toward the stairs.

"Don't move!" Kermit warned. "Don't get them excited!"

Evan froze. The tarantula prickled the top of his head. He watched in horror as the other one made its way across the lab table and began crawling up his arm.

Andy burst down the stairs, taking them two at a time. Her short brown hair bobbed behind her as she hurried across the basement to them.

Andy didn't dress like most sixth graders. She didn't care what other kids wore. She liked bright colors.

Today she wore a shiny magenta windbreaker over yellow tights. Her bright orange backpack hung over one shoulder.

"Hey, guys!" she greeted them breathlessly. "What are you doing?"

"An experiment," Kermit replied solemnly.

"So what else is new!" Andy said, rolling her eyes. But then her mouth dropped open in shock. She pointed at Evan with a trembling finger. "Evan! You have a tarantula on your head!"

Evan felt the creature dig into his hair.

15

"It's part of the experiment," Kermit told Andy. "There's another tarantula crawling on his arm."

"Get . . . them . . . off. . . ." Evan ordered Kermit through gritted teeth.

Andy laughed. "This is an awesome experiment!"

Evan let out a growl and raised his fists.

"Calm," Kermit warned. "If they sense your fear, you're dead meat."

Evan turned to Andy for help. But she had unzipped her backpack and was digging inside.

The tarantula prickled his scalp as it moved toward his left ear. "Kermit . . . ," he begged.

Evan gasped as Andy pulled a blue plastic can from her backpack.

"Evan, look what I found!" Her dark eyes lit up. An evil grin spread across her face.

"Monster Blood!" Evan cried. "Where'd you get that?"

"Somewhere," Andy teased. She raised her hand to the lid and started to twist it off.

"No —!" Evan shrieked. He dove toward her, grabbing for the can. "Don't open it! Andy — *don't*!"

5

Andy pulled the can from Evan's reach.

And twisted it open.

"NOOOO!" Evan shrieked.

She tilted the can so that he could see inside.

Empty.

She laughed and tossed the can aside. "April Fools'!"

"But it isn't April!" Kermit declared.

Evan gulped — and felt something pinch his ear. The tarantula! The Monster Blood can had frightened him so much, he'd forgotten about the creatures crawling over his body.

"Uh-oh. Now you've excited them!" Kermit warned. "I think we're going to learn how painful a tarantula bite can be."

Evan froze. He signaled frantically with his eyes for Andy to help him.

"Okay, okay," she said finally. She stepped up to Evan and plucked the tarantula off his head.

"You're ruining the experiment!" Kermit protested.

Andy pulled the other tarantula off Evan's arm. She handed them to Kermit.

Grumbling to himself, Kermit dropped them into the glass jar. Then he scribbled some notes in a notebook.

Evan glared angrily at his cousin, clenching his hands into tight fists. The tarantulas were gone, but his skin still prickled. "Let's get the Super-Soakers," he growled.

He couldn't wait to drench Kermit. He wanted to soak the little freak, to make him sputter and choke and shiver and shake until he begged for mercy.

And then Evan would *really* let him have it!

"It's kind of cold out for a water fight," Kermit said.

"I don't care," Evan growled. "Let's go."

He turned to Andy. She swung her backpack away and zipped it before he could see what was inside.

"What else have you got in there?" Evan demanded. "More dumb jokes?"

She sneered. "That's for me to know and you to find out."

"Do you have more Monster Blood in there?" His voice cracked. "Do you have *real* Monster Blood?"

"That's for me to know and you to find out," she repeated, hugging the backpack to her side.

Maybe I'll soak her too, Evan thought. She's asking for it. "Come on outside," he told her. "You can just watch."

"Like I believe you," she replied, rolling her eyes again. "I'll wait in here and do my homework. No way am I getting wet."

Evan eyed the backpack intently. Did she have a real can of Monster Blood in there? Did she?

Please — let the answer be *no*! he prayed as he led Kermit to the backyard.

They filled their squirt-gun canisters from the garden hose behind the garage. And the chase was on.

Kermit ran. Evan fired first. The Super-Soaker sprayed a stream of water over Kermit's head.

Evan lowered the squirt gun, and the water stream bounced off the back of Kermit's down jacket.

Evan pumped hard and kept the water flowing, squeezing the trigger again. Again. He raised the spray and caught Kermit in the back of the neck.

Kermit let out a *yipe* as the cold water ran down his back.

He spun around. And shot a stream of water in Evan's direction.

Evan dropped to his knees on the grass. The water stream flew over him.

He pulled the trigger and sent water splashing down the front of Kermit's jacket.

"Yo! Hey —!" A booming voice made Evan spin around.

"Conan —!" Evan cried.

Kermit sent a spray of icy water into the back of Evan's head.

Evan jumped up and staggered forward. "Kermit — stop!" He caught his balance before he bumped into Conan.

"You trying to get my new sneakers wet?" Conan snarled.

"No. No way," Evan replied. He lowered his Super-Soaker to his side.

Kermit stepped up beside Evan. "Give us a break, Conan," Kermit said. "Evan isn't afraid of you!"

"Oh, yeah?" Conan replied menacingly.

"Evan says he can take you down any day," Kermit boasted.

"I did not say that!" Evan cried. "Kermit — what is your problem?"

He turned to Conan. "I didn't say that. Really. My cousin is a little mixed up. You know. From the fumes. All those chemicals he fools around with."

Conan shook his beefy head. "You guys are really asking for it," he muttered angrily. He took a step toward Evan.

Evan gulped. He felt his Super-Soaker move.

He turned — and saw that Kermit had reached behind him.

Kermit was pushing up Evan's squirt gun.

Before Evan could jerk it away, Kermit pulled the trigger.

And a stream of water poured out over Conan's new sneakers.

6

Conan let out an angry cry. And grabbed the front of Evan's coat.

"I — I didn't do it!" Evan sputtered.

"It came out of *your* squirt gun," Conan replied. His big hands tightened on the coat. He tugged, lifting Evan off the ground.

"What are you going to do?" Evan shrieked.

"Hey — what's up?" Andy came trotting out from the house.

Conan let Evan drop to the ground.

Evan stumbled but quickly caught his balance.

"Evan is teaching Conan a lesson," Kermit reported.

Evan gave his cousin a hard shove. "I'm warning you, Kermit. . . ."

Conan eyed Andy suspiciously. "What's in your hand?" he demanded.

Evan turned as Andy held up her hand. She gripped a small blue plastic can.

"No —!" Evan gasped. "Andy — is that the empty one?"

She shook her head, an evil grin on her face. "Not empty. This one is full."

Evan took a step back. "Get rid of it, Andy."

Kermit reached for the can. "It's the real stuff? Let me see it," he demanded eagerly.

"Are you crazy?" Evan cried. "Why did you bring that here, Andy? You know how dangerous it is."

Andy's brown eyes flashed excitedly. She didn't say a word. Instead, she raised the blue can and started to pull off the lid.

"Nooo!" Evan wailed. "Have you totally lost it?"

Andy grinned at him.

"Don't open it!" Evan pleaded. "Please — don't open it!"

With a grunt, Conan stepped forward and swiped the can from Andy. "Let me see this stuff," he growled.

He raised the can in front of his face — and pulled off the lid.

7

Conan pulled open the lid — and three cloth snakes sprung out and hit him in the face.

He let out a startled yelp and let the can fall from his hand.

Andy tossed back her head and roared with laughter. Kermit laughed too, a high, shrill whinny.

Evan swallowed hard. Too shaken to laugh.

No one ever played jokes on Conan. *No one.*

Evan stared hard at Conan, frozen in terror. Conan's face was bright red. He was actually blushing!

Now he's going to *pound* us, Evan thought. When Conan is finished with us, we're going to look just like those three fake snakes on the ground.

But to Evan's surprise, Conan spun around and stomped off without saying a word.

"That was a close one," Evan murmured.

"It was funny!" Andy exclaimed. "What's your problem? Lose your sense of humor?"

"Yes," Evan told her. "I don't think Monster Blood is funny. It turned my dog, Trigger, into a giant. It turned our classroom hamster into a roaring monster. And it turned me into a twelve-foot-tall freak! That was the worst day of my life!"

"I saved you — remember? I shrank you back to your real size," Kermit bragged.

"Yes, you did," Evan had to admit. "That was the last good thing you ever did."

Kermit pouted. "That's not a nice thing to say, Evan. I shared my tarantulas with you — didn't I?"

Evan groaned in reply.

Kermit's expression suddenly changed. Behind his glasses, his eyes flashed. "Wait right here," he told them. He took off, running to his house.

"Where are you going now?" Evan called after him.

"I almost forgot what I wanted to show you," Kermit called back. "It's the coolest thing!"

He disappeared into the house.

Evan turned to Andy. "How am I going to survive ten days with him?" he wailed. "I just got here. And I've already had tarantulas climbing on my head!"

Andy laughed. "It could have been worse."

"How could it be worse?"

"Well . . . it could have been head lice," she said. "Remember when Kermit was collecting head lice?"

"You're not cheering me up, Annnnndrea," Evan groaned.

"Don't call me Andrea," she grumbled. "Wow. You're in a bad mood. Just think of all the money you are earning. Your aunt is paying you five dollars an hour to keep an eye on him — right?"

"If I survive," Evan moaned.

He turned to the house. Kermit came running across the grass, carrying a glass case between his hands.

"*Now* what is he bringing?" Evan cried.

"Maybe this is the head lice," Andy said.

"Will you please stop talking about head lice?" Evan pleaded. "You're making my head itch!"

"Check this out!" Kermit cried, holding the glass case up to them.

Evan squinted into the case. He saw white mice inside. Six or eight of them. With tiny black eyes and twitching pink noses. Crawling all over each other.

"Kermit — why did you bring your white mice outside?" he demanded.

"Watch," Kermit replied.

He pulled off the lid and dumped all the mice onto the grass.

The mice didn't hesitate. They scampered off in all directions. One of them ran right between Andy's legs. She cried out in surprise and leaped out of the way.

"Are you *crazy?*" Evan shrieked. "Your mice are all getting away!"

"No, they're not," Kermit replied calmly. He pulled a small gray control unit from the back pocket of his baggy jeans. It looked a lot like a TV remote control.

"This is so cool!" Kermit exclaimed. "See? I built an electric fence all the way around the backyard."

"I don't see any fence," Andy said.

"Of course not. It's electric," Kermit told her. "It's like the invisible fences people use to keep their dogs in the yard."

Evan squinted to the back of the yard. "I can't even see your mice anymore," he told Kermit. "They've all run away."

"No way," Kermit insisted. He raised the slender control unit. "I have electric current going all around the yard. If a mouse tries to go through it, he gets a mild shock."

"But they're gone!" Andy laughed. "The mice are all gone!"

Kermit gazed around the backyard.

His mouth dropped open. He slapped his fore-head. "Oh, wow! I forgot to turn the fence on! I forgot to throw the switch!"

He raised the control unit and pushed a red button.

"YAAAIIIIII!" Evan let out a scream as a jolt of electricity shot through his body.

Evan's arms waved wildly. His legs wiggled and bent.

Kermit pushed the red button again. The buzzing stopped.

Kermit stared at Evan. "Sorry. Guess you shouldn't be standing there."

Evan took a deep breath and held it. He waited for his skin to stop tingling.

"You looked like you were dancing!" Andy exclaimed. She threw her arms up and wiggled her body, imitating Evan.

"Am I supposed to think that's funny?" Evan asked weakly.

"Are you okay?" she asked. "Your hair is standing straight up on end!"

Evan pushed his hair down with both hands. But it popped right back up.

He glared at Kermit. "Any other great inventions?"

"Not right now," Kermit replied. "You have to help me."

"Help you do what?" Evan growled.

"Round up my mice," Kermit said. He began crawling across the grass on his hands and knees. "Hurry! They are expensive lab mice. Mom will kill me if I lose them."

Evan and Andy saw they had no choice. They dropped to their hands and knees and began crawling like Kermit.

"I don't see any mice," Evan whispered to Andy. "I think Kermit is in major trouble."

He heard a heavy thumping sound behind him. He turned and saw Dogface, the big sheepdog, bouncing across the yard.

"No, Dogface!" Kermit cried. "No! Go home! Go home!"

Furiously wagging his stubby tail, the big dog leaped onto Evan, sending him sprawling on the grass.

"Dogface — you're scaring the mice away!" Kermit wailed.

Ignoring Kermit's desperate pleas, the dog made a wide circle, excitedly running round and round the yard, barking and wagging his tail.

"Hey — what's going on?" an angry voice called. "Can't you keep that dog quiet?"

Conan came leaping over the low bushes that separated the two yards. Then he ran about three steps — and stopped.

Evan heard a crackling sound. Then a loud
BUZZ.

Conan's eyes bulged. His hands shot up. His
body twisted in a wild dance.

"Oh, wow," Kermit murmured. "Didn't I shut
that off?"

He fumbled with the control unit. The buzzing
stopped.

Conan took a few seconds to catch his breath.

Then he let out a furious roar. And dove at
Evan.

"Wh-what are you going to do to me?" Evan
stammered.

9

Evan leaned his elbows on the dinner table and stared down at the pile of spaghetti on his plate. Aunt Dee *couldn't* mess up spaghetti — could she? he wondered.

"Evan — what happened to your ear?" Aunt Dee asked.

Evan sighed. His left ear was normal. But his right ear throbbed and burned. He knew it must look like a red cabbage!

"What on earth happened to you?" his aunt demanded.

Evan didn't want to describe how Conan had won a tug-of-war with his ear. He mumbled something into his plate.

"Evan got into another fight with Conan," Kermit told his mom.

She lowered her fork. "Evan — is that true?"

Evan nodded. "It wasn't exactly a fight."

"I warned you to stay away from that boy," his

aunt scolded. "You really should be smart enough not to pick a fight with someone so big."

"And Evan lost all my white mice too," Kermit whined.

His mother's mouth dropped open. "Those mice cost a lot of money!" She narrowed her eyes at Evan.

Evan swallowed hard. "I'm not the one who brought them outside," he choked out.

"I left you in charge," Kermit's mom said sternly. "You are responsible for what goes on here when I'm away." She scowled and waved her fork at him. "If it's too big a job for you, Evan, I can find a grownup to come stay with Kermit."

"No!" Evan cried.

Being responsible for Kermit was *impossible*. But he didn't want to lose the job. If he didn't earn money, he couldn't go to sleepaway camp.

"I can handle the job," he told his aunt.

Across from him, Kermit gobbled down mouthful after mouthful of spaghetti. The orange sauce ran down his chin.

Evan rolled several spaghetti strands on his fork, then took a big bite.

He chewed for about three seconds. Then he let out a scream. "YAAAAAAIIIII!"

His mouth was on fire! His head felt about to explode!

"Is it spicy enough?" Aunt Dee asked. "Did I put in enough hot sauce?"

Later, as Evan changed into his pajamas, Kermit typed away on his computer. Evan's lips were swollen from the spicy spaghetti. They looked like two big salamis hanging from his face.

He gazed at himself in the dresser mirror. His ear resembled a red cabbage.

He shook his head unhappily, thinking about Conan. "I have to do something about him," he mumbled.

Kermit spun around from his keyboard. "What did you say?"

"Conan went too far this time," Evan grumbled bitterly. "He's making me look like a freak."

"Yes, you do," Kermit agreed.

"Shut up. I didn't ask you," Evan snapped. "You're not exactly Brad Pitt!"

"Who's that?" Kermit asked.

Evan ignored him. He climbed into bed. He hit the pillow a few times, fluffing it up. He knew he wouldn't be able to sleep.

He was too angry.

"This time Conan went too far," he repeated, muttering to himself. "This time I have to find a way to pay him back."

Behind his red-framed glasses, Kermit's round black eyes lit up. "You mean *revenge*?" he asked excitedly.

"Yeah. I guess," Evan replied, settling his huge ear on the pillow. His hands were clenched into tight fists. His whole body felt tense.

"Revenge." He repeated the word a few times. "That's what I want. Someone has to show Conan that he cannot keep pushing everyone around and beating everyone up. Revenge . . ."

Kermit shut off his computer. When he turned back to Evan, he had a wide grin on his face. "I think I can help you," he said.

10

"Let me show you something," Kermit said eagerly, lowering his voice to a whisper. He pulled something out of his bottom desk drawer and brought it over to Evan's foldout bed.

"Look." Kermit's grin grew wider. He handed the object to Evan.

"Hey —!" Evan cried out. "It's so hairy!"

Evan stared at the small object. Some kind of ball, covered in thick, greasy black hair. "This is totally gross," he told Kermit. "What is this? Why are you showing it to me?"

"It's an egg," Kermit said, giggling.

"Huh?" Evan nearly dropped it. He turned the hairy thing between his hands. "What kind of egg?" he asked suspiciously.

"Just an egg," Kermit replied. "I took it from the refrigerator."

"But —" Evan started.

"Remember, I told you about my hair-growing

formula?" Kermit asked. "I said it wasn't ready yet. But it is."

Evan handed the hairy egg back to his cousin. It was too creepy. It was making him sick.

He swallowed. "You really can grow thick hair like that on an egg?"

Kermit nodded, grinning. He cradled the egg in his hands as if it were a precious jewel. "My hair mixture works, Evan. We can use it to pay Conan back."

"Whoa!" Evan cried. "We can't make him drink it and turn his mouth all hairy. That's too horrible — even for Conan."

"I know," Kermit agreed. "But we can pour it on his hands, can't we? We can give him werewolf hands! That would be pretty funny — wouldn't it?"

Evan laughed. "Yeah. Yeah, it sure would! Let's do it!"

Kermit carried the hairy egg back to his desk drawer. "I was going to test my hair mixture out on Dogface next," he told Evan. "But Dogface is already hairy enough. Conan is better."

"Much better," Evan agreed, smiling for the first time that night. "Where is your hair mixture?"

"Don't worry. I have it hidden safe and sound," Kermit replied. "It will be ready when we need it."

It took Evan hours to fall asleep. Partly because he couldn't stop thinking of his revenge against Conan. And partly because Kermit was snoring his head off.

Evan stared up at the ceiling with his hands over his ears, unable to shut out the awful sound. A throaty *gluggg glugggg*, followed by a whistle.

Kermit is obnoxious even when he's asleep, Evan thought bitterly.

When he finally fell asleep, Evan dreamed he was standing in his pajamas in Kermit's backyard. It was night. Long shadows fell over the grass.

Peering into the back of the yard, Evan saw Kermit's white mice. At least half a dozen of them. They had clustered around something hidden in the grass.

In the dream, Evan moved closer. And saw what had interested the lab mice.

A blue can. An open can of Monster Blood!

Evan's mouth dropped open in horror.

The green gunk had bubbled out of the can. And the white mice were silently gobbling it. Gobbling down chunk after chunk. Their teeth gnashing up and down. Their furry bodies quivering with excitement as they ate.

As they swallowed down the sticky green goo,

they grew. Evan stared in shock. The mice inflated until they were as big as dogs. Then bigger. The giant mice rose up on their hind legs.

They're taller than *me*! Evan saw, stumbling back. And so fat! They must weigh two hundred pounds!

They turned to him, gnashing their teeth hungrily. As tall as the house, the mice lurched heavily toward Evan.

One of them tossed back its head, opened its jaws wide, and let out a roar. Evan saw rows of jagged gray teeth.

And then the mice lurched heavily toward him. Their feet thudded the ground. Their dark eyes glinted in the silvery glow from the moon.

"Noooooooooo!" He opened his mouth in a long, high howl.

He raised his hands to protect himself.

The mice rose over him now. One of them lowered its head. Its jagged teeth slid around Evan's waist. Its jaw tightened.

Evan felt its hot, sour breath stream over him.

Felt the teeth dig into his side.

And then he was being lifted up. Lifted in the giant jaws of the white mouse. The mouse clamped its jaws shut. Bit down hard.

Evan knew it was chewing him. Chewing him to pieces.

He opened his eyes. Began to lift himself from

the frightening dream. Lift himself . . . lift himself . . .

And heard a tapping at Kermit's bedroom window.

Evan squinted through the darkness. To the window. And saw a giant mouse!

11

No.

No. The mouse was part of the dream.

I'm still half in my dream, half awake, Evan realized, blinking his eyes.

He shook himself hard. Shook himself awake.

The mouse faded slowly, then vanished. And Evan stared at the window, stared at Andy outside in the darkness. Tapping on the glass. Tapping so urgently.

Evan jumped from the small foldout bed. His legs were tangled in the blanket. He stumbled and had to grab the edge of Kermit's dresser to catch his balance.

One foot had fallen asleep. He dragged it, limping to the window. He silently pushed open the window, careful not to wake Kermit.

Kermit snored away, *glugging* and whistling. He had kicked his blanket to the floor. He had fallen asleep with his glasses on.

Evan leaned out into the darkness. A gust of cold wind made him shiver.

"Andy — what are you doing here?" he cried out."

"Get dressed," Andy ordered. "Hurry, Evan. I have to show you something."

"Huh?" He glanced back at Kermit's clock radio. "It's almost midnight!"

Andy raised a finger to her lips. "Sssshhhh. Hurry. Get dressed. I think you'll want to see this."

She held up a can. A blue plastic can.

Evan groaned. "You really came here in the middle of the night for another joke? Give me a break, Andy. What's going to spring out at me *this* time?"

But then he saw the serious expression on Andy's face.

"It isn't a joke — is it?" he whispered.

She shook her head.

"It's Monster Blood — right?" Evan demanded.

Andy nodded. "I think so. The can — it looks the same."

Evan spun away from the window. He pulled on jeans and a sweatshirt right over his pajamas. His hands trembled as he tied his shoes.

He grabbed his down jacket from the closet. And climbed out the window.

"I was dreaming about Monster Blood," he told Andy.

She bit her bottom lip. "This isn't a dream," she replied quietly.

Evan shivered. It was a cold, clear night.

Andy wore her magenta windbreaker and a pair of silvery leggings. She had a red wool ski cap pulled down over her short brown hair.

She raised the plastic can to Evan. "I think it's the real thing. I hurried over as soon as I was sure my parents were asleep."

"Where did you get it?" he whispered.

"Behind the lab on Peachtree where my dad works. We were picking him up before dinner. I was waiting in the parking lot behind the lab. I found this in a whole pile of stuff."

"You didn't open it — did you?" Evan demanded.

"No way," she replied. She tried to hand him the can. But he waved it away.

"I don't want it," Evan told her. "Why did you bring it over here?"

Andy shrugged. "I thought after this afternoon, you might want to pay Conan back for being such a big jerk."

"Yes, I do want to pay Conan back," Evan admitted.

"So use the Monster Blood," Andy urged. "You can put a little of it in his lunch at school. You can —"

"No way!" Evan cried. "Conan is already a *mountain*! I don't want to make him any BIG-GER!"

The light faded from Andy's dark eyes. "I guess you're right. But we could put Monster Blood in his bed. Or —"

"Stop!" Evan ordered. "It's too dangerous. I don't want to use Monster Blood on Conan. Kermit and I have another plan for Conan. A really good plan."

"What is it?" Andy demanded eagerly.

"I'll tell you as soon as you get rid of the Monster Blood," Evan told her. "I really don't want that stuff around. Go hide it someplace where no one will ever find it."

"But, Evan —" Andy protested.

Evan didn't let her finish. "You know what will happen if that can gets opened," he said firmly. "It will bubble up. And it will grow and grow, and we won't be able to stop it."

"Okay, okay." Andy rolled her eyes. "I'll take it home. I'll find a good hiding place."

"Promise?" Evan demanded, eyeing her sharply.

"Promise," she repeated, raising her right hand.

"Hey — what's that?" a voice called from behind them.

Evan spun around and saw Kermit scramble out the open window.

44

Kermit grabbed the blue can from Andy's hand.

"Cool!" he cried. "Monster Blood! Is it real?"

He didn't wait for an answer.

He gripped the can tightly — and pulled off the lid.

12

"No! Don't do that!" Evan screamed.

Too late.

"Close it up!" Evan cried frantically. "Close the can — quick!"

Kermit stood staring into the open can. "It's too dark. I can't see anything."

"Give me that!" Evan ordered. He leaped forward and tried to swipe the can away.

He grabbed the can — but knocked the lid from Kermit's hand.

Kermit made a wild grab for the lid. But a gust of wind blew it out of his reach.

As Evan gaped in horror, the wind lifted the plastic lid . . . lifted it over their heads.

"Noooooo!" He let out a long wail as the lid spun crazily above them. He made a wild grab. Another. Missed.

The wind carried the lid up to the slanted roof of the house. It hit the shingles. Slid down a few feet. And came to a rest in the metal rain gutter.

"I don't believe this," Evan muttered.

"I'll get the ladder from the garage," Kermit offered. He took off across the dew-wet grass.

"Hurry!" Evan cried.

"The Monster Blood — it's moving!" Andy exclaimed, pointing with a trembling finger.

Evan gazed down at the can gripped tightly in his hand. He couldn't really see inside. Dark clouds had drifted over the moon, blocking out the light.

Evan brought the can close to his face. And gasped.

"Andy — it's *blue*!"

"Huh?" She pressed close to him. Their heads banged as they both eagerly stared into the can.

Yes. The thick glop inside the can was blue — not green.

It made a sick *plopping* sound as it rolled from side to side, like an ocean wave.

"It — it's trying to get out!" Andy stammered.

"Hurry, Kermit!" Evan called.

Kermit came running from the garage, an aluminum ladder tilted over one shoulder.

"Why is it blue?" Andy asked.

The thick goo lapped at the side of the can. As Evan stared in horror, it splashed up over the top.

"Kermit — please hurry! Get the lid!" he cried.

Kermit propped the ladder against the side of the house. Then he turned back to them. "Someone else has to climb up," he called.

"Just *do* it!" Evan screamed frantically. "The stuff is spilling out over the top!"

"But I'm afraid of heights!" Kermit declared.

Evan rolled his eyes. "It isn't that high. Just climb up, and —"

"I can't!" Kermit whined. "Really!"

"I'll do it." Andy ran to the ladder. Kermit held it steady for her.

Evan watched her scramble up. The Monster Blood bobbed and plopped in the can. The clouds rolled away from the moon. It was definitely bright blue, Evan saw.

And ·definitely trying to raise itself out of the can.

Andy climbed up to the gutter. Holding the ladder with her right hand, she reached out to the lid with her free hand.

Reached . . . reached . . .

And the wind blew the lid from the gutter.

"Noooo —!" Andy screamed. She grabbed for it.

Lost her balance.

Grabbed the sides of the ladder with both hands.

The lid spun crazily in the air. Then it swooped down to the grass.

"I've got it!" Kermit cried. He dove for it and grabbed it in one hand.

"Yes!" Evan cried happily. "Put it on the can — quick!"

Andy carefully lowered herself rung by rung.

She reached the ground, turned, breathing hard, and hurried back to Evan.

Kermit came running over with the lid.

But before he reached Evan, a voice rang out from the yard across from his.

"Hey — what's going on?"

Evan looked up to see Conan running across the grass.

"Oh, no!" Evan moaned, and the Monster Blood can fell out of his hand.

13

With a gasp, Evan bent to pick up the can.

Had the blue Monster Blood spilled out?

No.

He lifted it carefully, holding one hand over the open top.

Conan stopped at the edge of the yard. "What are you three babies doing out so late?" he demanded. "I'll tell your mommies!"

"Give us a break, Conan," Andy called. "We're not bothering you!"

"Your *face* is bothering me!" Conan shot back. Then his eyes fell on the can in Evan's hand. "What's that?"

Evan nearly dropped the can again. "This? Uh . . . nothing. . . . It's . . ."

Evan's mind went blank. He couldn't think of a good lie to tell Conan.

Kermit grabbed the can away from Evan. "It's candy," he told Conan. "Blue Fruit Roll in a Barrel! We saw it on TV, and it's awesome."

"Give me some!" Conan ordered. He reached out his big hand.

"No way!" Kermit teased him, pulling the can back. "We're not sharing with you!"

He pretended to lick the blue candy. "Wow. That's really excellent!"

"Guess I'm going to have to take it from you," Conan declared menacingly. He took a step toward them, his hand outstretched. "Give it."

"Are you crazy?" Evan whispered to Kermit. "Why did you tease him? Now he's going to take it and —"

"No problem," Kermit whispered back. A sly grin spread over his face. "Watch."

"Give it," Conan thundered, waving his outstretched hand. He took another step toward them. Another.

Evan heard the crackle of electricity before he saw the white spark.

Conan's eyes bulged. His hands shot up. His knees buckled.

"Urg. Urg." He uttered two strange cries as Kermit's invisible electric fence zapped him again.

Conan staggered back, gasping for breath. His broad chest heaved up and down. He reminded Evan of a bull about to charge.

Kermit raised the can and pretended to eat the Monster Blood again. "Wow. That is *excellent!*" he declared.

Conan glared at the three of them. Even across

the dark yard, Evan could see the fury on his face.

But the bull couldn't charge. Couldn't get to them. Not as long as the electric fence was turned on.

Conan balled his hands into fists. "You're history," he called to them. "All three of you. You're roadkill."

He spun around. Swinging his fists hard at his sides, he stomped into his house.

Andy let out a sigh of relief. "That was pretty good!" she told Kermit.

A high, shrill giggle escaped Kermit's throat. "Yeah. Not bad!"

"There's just one problem," Evan murmured. "We're roadkill if we ever leave this backyard!"

He turned to Kermit. "Give me back the can. We'd better close it —"

Evan gasped.

The can in Kermit's hand! He was holding it upside down!

Evan grabbed for it.

Too late.

With a sick *PLOP*, the blue gunk dropped out of the can.

It landed on the grass in front of Evan's feet. He stared down at it as it quivered. Quivered and shook, like blue Jell-O.

It glowed in the light from the moon. Glowed bright blue.

Bobbed and trembled.

And grew.

"It's . . . changing shape!" Andy cried. She leaned forward, resting her hands on her knees, and gazed down wide-eyed at it.

The blue blob wiggled. It rolled over once, moving away from Evan.

And grew some more.

It rolled again. Wiggled from side to side.

And then rose up. Up . . . as if trying to stand.

"I don't *believe* this!" Evan choked out. "It's some kind of *creature*!"

"You're right!" Kermit agreed. "It's ALIVE!"

14

Evan squatted on the grass, watching the blue Monster Blood intently. Andy and Kermit stood openmouthed as the creature bounced, and grew, and took shape.

A sleek blue head popped up from the body. A curved gash in the head became a mouth. It turned up in a goofy grin.

Two big, round eyes appeared above the mouth.

The creature was about the size of.a chipmunk. It made a squeaking sound as it bounced over the grass. Its rubbery body throbbed rapidly, like a heart.

"It's so cute!" Andy declared, raising her hands to the sides of her face. "It's like a lovable little blob creature."

"It looks friendly," Kermit added. "It keeps staring up at us and smiling."

Evan didn't say a word. As he studied the creature, a heavy feeling of dread formed in the pit of his stomach.

I don't care how cute the little guy looks, he thought. This is Monster Blood. And Monster Blood is always evil.

"Let's try to push it back in the can," he suggested.

The creature bounced and squeaked.

"Do you think it will fit?" Kermit asked.

Evan stared at the grinning blob. "We have to squeeze it back in," he told them.

"But it's so cute!" Andy protested. She bent down close to the little creature. "You're a cute guy, aren't you?" she said to it. "Do you like to be petted?"

Andy reached for it with both hands.

It slid right through her fingers and bounced away, squeaking loudly.

"Oooh! It's so cold and wet!" Andy declared. "Look! It's like a little seal!"

She made another grab for it. But again the blobby creature bounced away from her.

Kermit stepped in front of it. "I'd like to get it under a microscope," he said. "Maybe take a few tissue samples."

"You have to catch it first," Evan told him.

Kermit dove for it. Grabbed.

The creature bounced over his hands and escaped.

"Hey — he licked me!" Kermit exclaimed. "I think he licked me."

"He seems to be friendly," Andy said. She

dropped to her knees. "Here, Blobby. Here, Blobby," she called. She held out her hands to it.

To everyone's surprise, the creature bounced over to her.

Andy trapped it gently between her hands. She giggled. "It's so *cold!*"

She ran her hand tenderly over the back of its quivering body. "Do you like to be petted?" she asked it again softly.

The creature purred.

Evan and Kermit both let out cries of surprise.

Andy petted the blue blob some more. It purred louder.

"He likes it!" Andy declared, laughing.

"Weird," Kermit murmured. "See if you can pull off a hunk so I can study it."

"No way!" Andy cried. "You're not hurting my little Blobby." She petted it tenderly.

"Be careful," Evan warned. "This is Monster Blood — remember?"

"It can't be," Andy argued. "Monster Blood is green. This cute thing is something else."

"It might be a different kind of Monster Blood," Kermit suggested. "You know. A different flavor."

"Whoa!" Andy cried out as the creature bounced. out of her hands. Throbbing wetly, it began bouncing and rolling toward the garage.

"Catch it!" Evan cried.

All three of them chased after the creature. It moved surprisingly fast.

Kermit made a grab for it — and it slid through his hands.

Evan ran in front of it and tried to block its path. But it rolled around him and kept bouncing.

"Don't let it get away!" Andy cried.

Evan made another frantic grab — and lifted the wet blob off the ground. "Got it!" Evan cried.

But the creature changed shape. Squeaking loudly, it pulled itself in until it resembled a giant worm. And then it slid easily from Evan's hands.

"Whoa — it's *cold*!" Evan exclaimed. He examined his hands. The creature had left a coating of wet blue slime on Evan's palms.

Evan glanced up in time to see the creature roll to the back of the yard. "Stop it!" he cried. "Don't let it go over to Conan's yard!"

He ran to catch up to it. Kermit reached it first. "Hey — what's it doing?" Kermit demanded. "It's turning on the garden hose."

The hose was coiled against the back of the garage. A long end of it stretched along the ground.

Evan stopped and stared as the creature perched on top of the nozzle. Its body began to bounce up and down in a steady rhythm. It stopped squeaking and began to make loud gulping sounds.

"Is it drinking?" Andy asked.

"Huh? I think it is!" Evan cried, staring in amazement.

The creature bobbed on top of the hose nozzle. Drinking. And as it drank, it grew.

"It's inflating — like a water balloon!" Kermit declared.

"We'd better stop it before it gets too big," Evan warned.

Evan tried to turn the water off, but the spigot wouldn't budge. "It's stuck!" he cried. "I can't turn it! It's stuck!"

The creature gulped more water. It was as big as a basketball now, and still growing.

Evan grabbed it with both hands and tugged. His hands slid off the slippery, wet body.

The creature was as big as a beach ball.

"Help me!" Evan cried, grabbing the creature again. "We've got to pull it off the hose."

He gave a hard tug. But the gulping creature held on to the hose.

Andy stepped up beside Evan. They both wrapped their arms around the inflating creature and struggled to pull it loose.

"It — it's attached itself!" Evan gasped.

The creature bulged, bigger, bigger, until Evan and Andy couldn't get their arms around it.

"Now what?" Evan groaned.

And the creature exploded.

Evan heard a deafening *POP*. A wave of cold water and slime hurtled over him, knocking him over.

Evan landed in a sitting position.

"Ohhhhh." He let out a groan as he wiped the thick blanket of slime off his eyes and face.

"Sick," he heard Andy mutter.

He turned and saw that Kermit and Andy were also drenched. Thick gobs of slime clung to Kermit's glasses. Andy's hair was soaked, matted flat on her head.

"Sick," Andy repeated, staring down at her slime-covered hands. "Oh, yuck. This is *sick*."

Evan wiped more goo from his eyes. Then he turned to where the creature had stood — and gasped in shock. "Oh, noooo!" he cried. "Am I *seeing* things?"

15

Two blue creatures bobbed beside the garage.

Two creatures about the size of chipmunks.

Squeaking softly, they grinned at Evan, Kermit, and Andy. Their big black eyes rolled in their heads.

"It *multiplied!*" Kermit exclaimed.

Evan swallowed hard. He scooped a gob of slime off his shoulder. "I don't like this," he murmured. "I don't like this one bit."

"But they're so cute!" Andy protested.

Evan shivered. The night air suddenly felt much colder. He turned to the house. It was covered in darkness.

What if Aunt Dee wakes up and catches us out here? he wondered. I'll be in major trouble. My baby-sitting job will be over. No sleepaway camp . . .

"It's getting late," he told them. "We've got to go in."

"But we can't just leave these little guys out here!" Andy protested.

Evan sighed. He knew Andy was right. "Okay," he agreed, "let's round them up quickly. We'll get a bag or a bucket or something."

The two blue blobs began bouncing in different directions.

"No! Don't let them get away!" Evan cried. "If they split up, we'll never catch them."

"I have an idea," Kermit said. He darted across the grass and picked up the garden hose. He turned the nozzle, and a hard spray shot out.

"I'll keep them against the back of the garage," he announced. "You go find something to put them in."

Evan watched as Kermit raised the hose and aimed the spray at the two creatures.

The hard spray sent them both flying against the garage wall.

"It's working!" Kermit cried. "I've trapped them!"

He kept the spray on them. The water pushed them back, pressing the two creatures against the garage.

"Hurry —!" Kermit cried.

But Evan hesitated. He watched as the two creatures opened their mouths wide. Wider. And began to gulp.

"Kermit — turn off the hose!" Evan shouted. "It's a bad idea. They're *drinking* it!"

As the stream of water shot into their gaping mouths, the creatures inflated rapidly. They gulped the water hungrily, blowing up bigger and bigger.

"Kermit — shut off the hose!" Evan ordered.

Too late.

Another loud explosion. Another burst of water and slime.

And now Evan stared across the lawn at FOUR blue blobs!

Startled, Kermit dropped the hose. Water shot across the lawn.

Evan dove for the garage and frantically turned the water spigot. The water dribbled to a stop.

But the four blue creatures were already lapping up water from the grass. And growing bigger.

"We have to stop them," Evan gasped. "We have to pick them up before they explode again."

He and Andy ran together, frantically reaching down to grab two of them. But Andy stopped suddenly — and Evan ran right into her.

"Whoa!" he cried. "Why did you stop?"

"Look at them." Andy pointed.

Evan gazed down at the bobbing creatures. They were lapping the night dew off the grass. "What about them?" he asked impatiently.

"These four look different," Andy replied. "Check out their faces. They're not smiling."

"Who cares?" Evan shrieked. "They're *drinking*! Why do we care if they're smiling or not? Do we want *eight* of them? No! So let's get them!"

Evan leaped forward and grabbed one in each hand. One blue blob slipped out and bounced away, squeaking loudly.

Evan wrapped both hands around the other one, determined to hold it tight. "Get a bucket!" he told Andy. "Or a garbage bag or something!"

Then Evan let out a scream as a sharp jolt of pain shot through his arm.

He looked down. The blue creature had clamped its jaws around his wrist.

"H-help!" Evan stammered. "Owwwww! It — it's *biting* me! It's biting my hand off!"

16

Evan tugged at the creature with his free hand. "Help me! Ow! It — it's sucking my skin!" he wailed.

Kermit and Andy dove to his side. They both grabbed at the wet blue blob. Andy's hands slipped off, and she stumbled backwards.

But Kermit held on, held on with both hands. And tugged. Tugged until they all heard a loud *POP*.

Kermit pulled the creature off and tossed it across the yard.

Evan rubbed his arm. "It was sucking my skin," he moaned. "Sucking the water out, I guess."

Kermit started running to the house. "I'm telling Mom," he cried. "This is too dangerous!"

"No!" Evan grabbed Kermit around the waist. "I can't get·in any more trouble with your mom. Let's get them all rounded up first. If we don't, there will be *hundreds* of them!"

Evan turned to Andy. Her teeth were chattering. "This is getting scary," she murmured. "Listen to them."

The blue blobs weren't grinning anymore. Low growls came out of their scowling mouths.

"They were so cute," Andy said softly. "But now they're turning mean."

Two of the creatures were rolling in the grass, sucking up moisture. Two others were bouncing toward the garden hose.

Evan turned away. He glanced quickly to the house. "Where is Kermit?" he asked.

Andy shrugged. "Did he go inside to tell his mother?"

"I hope not," Evan moaned. "I'm going to be in such bad trouble!"

The blue blobs were inflating, getting ready to explode and multiply.

"I'm *already* in big trouble," Evan told himself. He started to the house. But halfway there, he saw Kermit running from the garage.

"I'll catch them!" Kermit cried. He waved a long-handled net in the air. Evan recognized it — the net Kermit used to collect butterflies.

Kermit ran across the grass, swinging the net.

Evan heard a loud, wet explosion. His eyes swept over the dark lawn. How many were there now?

Eight?

Yes.

His throat tightened in panic. *We can't catch them all!* he thought.

65

Kermit lowered the net to the grass. Swung hard. And captured one of the blue blobs.

It uttered a sharp growl. The net bounced and shook at the end of its pole.

"Got one! Where do I dump it?" Kermit called excitedly.

Evan spotted a bucket at the side of the garage. He ran across the grass toward it, waving to Kermit to follow him.

Kermit saw the bucket too. He began to lower the net into it. "In you go!" he cried.

But they both heard a ripping sound.

The creature hurtled out from the net — and bounced away.

"He — he chewed through the net!" Kermit exclaimed. He tossed the net aside.

Evan picked up the bucket and chased after the bouncing creature. "Just pick them up and toss them in," he cried. "If we can keep them from drinking, they won't multiply."

Andy dove for one. It slipped out of her hands. "We need gloves," she suggested. "We could hold them better if —"

"We don't have time to find gloves!" Evan cried. "If we don't catch them fast, there will be a *hundred* of them!"

"But what if they grab on to you?" Andy cried. "What if they start sucking your skin?"

Evan didn't know how to answer that question. He swallowed hard. "Just be careful," he told her.

Hearing low grunts, he raised his eyes to Aunt Dee's flower garden. "Oh, noooo!" he moaned.

"Mom's flowers!" Kermit cried.

Three or four of the creatures were sucking the water from the flowers. The blobs were already huge, ready to explode. A wide path of flowers lay dead and wilted behind them.

Kermit's mother took such pride in her flower garden; she struggled to keep it blooming all through the winter. And now it's a mess, Evan saw.

And she's going to blame me.

"Get them!" he shouted. "Get them out of the flowers!"

But he heard a muffled scream. And spun around.

"Help me . . . help . . ." Andy struggled as a big blue blob wrapped around her face.

It pulsed and throbbed.

She hit it with both fists. Pounded it.

She dropped to her knees, struggling to remove it.

Evan froze in horror as the creature grunted and growled, spreading wetly over Andy's face.

"Help . . . ," she moaned. "Can't breathe . . . can't breathe . . ."

17

Evan gasped in horror as Andy struggled with the blue creature. She pounded it with her fists. Pulled at its slippery skin. Shoved it with her open palms.

Evan took a deep breath. Ran over to her. And grasped the creature in both hands.

It's so slippery and cold! he thought.

He dug his fingers into its wet flesh, tightening his grip.

Then he heaved up with all his strength.

The creature lifted off Andy's face with a loud *POP*. Evan lost his balance and nearly fell.

The blob slipped out of his hands, bounced over the grass, and landed in a large puddle near the driveway.

"Ohhhhhh, sick!" Andy moaned. She wiped thick slime off her face. Still on her knees, her whole body trembled.

Evan raised his eyes to the blob. Facedown, it

gulped the puddle noisily. Its shimmery blue body bulged bigger, bigger . . .

Until it exploded — sending a wave of water and slime over Evan and Andy. Evan staggered back as the cold gunk washed over him.

Wiping it off his eyes, he helped Andy to her feet.

"The flowers!" Kermit cried. "They've ruined them all!"

Evan turned to the garden. In time to see two more inflated blue blobs explode into four.

The four new blobs bounced up and down furiously, gnashing their pointed teeth.

"The new ones have teeth!" Andy declared. "Each time they explode, they get meaner!"

"I've had enough of this!" Evan exclaimed. He grabbed a shovel on the ground beside the flower garden. "Kermit, Andy — hurry! Get big trash bags!"

Kermit darted into the garage. A few seconds later, he came out carrying two plastic trash bags. He handed one to Andy. They swung them open and ran to catch up with Evan.

"Let's get these guys!" Evan declared.

He lowered the shovel blade to the ground and scooped up a blue blob.

Andy held out her trash bag. Evan dropped the creature into the bag. It plopped in heavily. Andy gripped the top of the bag and held on.

Working feverishly, Evan scooped up another one and dropped it into Andy's bag.

Another explosion sent a wave of slime flying. Evan ducked under it — and caught *two* blue blobs on his shovel blade. With a groan, he swung the blade hard into Kermit's trash bag.

In minutes, the two trash bags bulged.

"Only a few left," Evan said, catching his breath. Despite the cool night air, sweat poured down his forehead.

Beside the garage, two creatures gulped water hungrily from a puddle on the grass. Another creature bounced over the wilted flower garden, uttering low, angry growls.

"These guys are trying to get out," Kermit complained. He had hoisted his bag over his slender shoulder.

The bag throbbed. Inside it, the creatures grunted and growled.

"What are we going to do with these bags?" Andy demanded. "These blue things are *alive*! We can't just throw them in trash cans."

"They wouldn't fit, anyway," Kermit said.

Evan wiped sweat off his forehead with the back of his hand. "Let's get them all collected. first," he sighed. "Then we can decide what to do."

It took several minutes to round up the final three. They kept bouncing away and sliding off the shovel.

Finally, all of the grunting, growling creatures

were caught. Evan helped Kermit and Andy tie up the bulging trash bags.

"Now what?" Andy demanded.

Evan blinked as a bright yellow light flashed on. Another light.

The lawn shimmered green, nearly as bright as day. The colors all came into focus.

Evan spun toward the house. The porch light had been turned on. And all the lights around the yard.

"It's Mom!" Kermit gasped. "We're caught!"

18

Evan could see Aunt Dee in the kitchen, moving to the back door. "Quick — don't let her see! Hide the trash bags!" he cried.

"But where?" Kermit demanded.

"Just hide them!" Evan ordered.

Kermit and Andy grabbed up their bulging trash bags. Kermit led the way around the side of the house. "We'll drag them to the basement," he said. "I'll lock them in a storage closet or something. We can figure out what to do with them in the morning."

The back door swung open, and Aunt Dee stepped out onto the back stoop. She tightened her bathrobe belt and squinted around the yard.

"My garden!" she shrieked in horror, raising her hands to her face.

And then her eyes stopped on Evan.

"Huh?" she gasped. "Evan — what on earth are you doing out at this time of night?"

"Well . . ."

Evan's mind raced. He knew there was *no way* he could come up with a good explanation.

"My flowers —!" Aunt Dee cried.

"I . . . uh . . . I heard someone out here," Evan started. "But . . ."

I'm a terrible liar, he told himself. I'd better not even try to make up a story.

"Get in the house — this instant!" his aunt growled. "I'm going to have a long talk with your parents when they get back. I'm very disappointed in you, Evan. Very disappointed."

"Sorry," Evan gulped. He obediently slunk into the house.

Aunt Dee was talking angrily, scolding him, asking him what he was doing outside.

But he didn't hear her. He was thinking about the two bulging, throbbing bags of blue Monster Blood creatures in the basement.

We'll get rid of them in the morning, he told himself. Then everything will be okay. Right?

Right?

Right. He answered his own question.

Aunt Dee scolded Evan for a few minutes more. Kermit was already tucked into bed when Evan finally entered the darkened bedroom.

Evan stepped into the room and closed the door behind him. "Did you lock up the bags somewhere?" he whispered.

"No problem," Kermit replied sleepily. He yawned. "All safe and sound."

Evan got undressed quickly, letting his clothes fall to the floor. He began to feel sleepy too. The battle against the blue blobs had worn him out.

He sighed.

Tomorrow will be better, he thought. I'll be able to think more clearly in the morning. I'll figure out a way to get rid of all the Monster Blood creatures.

He pulled the covers down a few inches and slid into the foldout bed. He settled in. Rested his head on the pillow.

Then he felt the cold, wet creature on his back.

And he started to scream.

19

The dampness spread over the back of Evan's pajamas. The cold chilled him until his skin prickled.

He leaped up. Whirled around. Let out another cry as the lights flashed on.

He stared down at a wet washcloth on his sheet. And heard Kermit's high-pitched giggle.

"Kermit — you jerk!" Evan cried.

His cousin stood by the light switch, shaking with laughter.

"Kermit — do you really think this was the best time to play such a mean joke?" Evan demanded, his heart still pounding.

Kermit shrugged. "Guess not." Then he started giggling all over again.

Evan angrily grabbed up the cold, wet washcloth and heaved it at his cousin. "Let's get some sleep," he growled. "We have a lot to do tomorrow. And it's no joke."

* * *

Evan dreamed about blue balloons. There were dozens of them in the dream, and they grew bigger and bigger.

The balloons floated above him, their long strings hanging down. Evan tried to capture the balloons by grabbing the strings.

But as he held on, the strings turned into wriggling snakes.

Evan tried to let go, but the snakes wrapped around his hands. And the huge blue balloons lifted him off the ground and carried him higher and higher — until they popped.

And he woke up.

Morning sunlight washed into the bedroom. Evan felt tired and shaky, as if he hadn't slept at all. He glanced across the room at his cousin.

Kermit had kicked all his blankets off onto the floor. He slept at the foot of his bed, twisted like a pretzel.

He probably had bad dreams too, Evan thought.

He spotted the wet washcloth on the floor.

Good! Evan said to himself. Kermit *deserves* bad dreams!

But as he pulled on jeans and a sweatshirt, a heavy feeling of dread swept over Evan.

The Monster Blood creatures. They were down in the basement. Waiting.

How can we get rid of them? Evan asked himself. Should we tell Aunt Dee? Should we call the police?

He stared at himself in the mirror as he brushed his teeth. His eyes were bloodshot. He had dark circles around them.

He shook Kermit's shoulders and woke him up. "Huh?" Kermit groaned. He squinted hard at Evan, as if he didn't recognize him.

"Wake up," Evan ordered. "We have a job to do — remember?"

Kermit blinked several times. Without his big red glasses, his eyes looked tiny.

"We have to dump those trash bags somewhere," Evan reminded him.

"I have an idea," Kermit replied.

They hurried to the kitchen. Aunt Dee had left a note on the refrigerator. She went early to the garden store to buy new flowers for her garden. She told the boys to make cereal for breakfast.

But Evan didn't feel like eating. His stomach felt as if it were filled with lead.

"We'll eat after we take care of the blobs," he told Kermit.

Kermit nodded solemnly. He led the way to the basement stairs.

"Where did you hide the trash bags?" Evan asked as they started down the steps.

"I locked them in the little bathroom," Kermit replied.

"Huh?" Evan let out a gasp. He grabbed Kermit and spun him around. "Isn't there a sink in that bathroom? And a toilet? And water pipes?"

"Well . . . yeah," Kermit replied. "But the creatures are in bags — remember?"

"*Plastic* bags!" Evan reminded him. "They probably chewed through those bags in seconds!"

Kermit's mouth dropped open. "Do you think so?"

They stopped outside the bathroom door. Evan pressed his ear to the door, listening hard. "Uh-oh," he murmured. "I think I hear running water."

"Oh, wow." Kermit shook his head. "Oh, wow. Oh, wow. I just remembered something else."

"Something else?" Evan narrowed his eyes on his cousin. "What else did you just remember?"

Kermit swallowed. "Uh . . . well . . . I just remembered that this bathroom is where I hid the bottle that has my hair-growing formula."

"Oh, nooooo," Evan moaned.

"I didn't want anyone to find it," Kermit explained. "No one ever uses this bathroom. So I hid it in here."

Evan pressed his ear to the bathroom door again. He reached for the knob.

"No — don't!" Kermit cried.

"We have no choice," Evan told him.

He pulled open the door.

20

"Oh, nooooo!" Evan screamed.

He tried to slam the door shut. But Monster Blood creatures bounced into the doorway, blocking the door.

"There are *hundreds* of them!" Kermit shrieked. "And — and they're all *hairy*!"

As the big blobs bounced past the two boys into the basement, Evan gaped into the little bathroom in shock.

Dozens and dozens of the blobs bounced and drank and growled and chomped their pointy teeth. Their sleek blue skin was now covered in thick tufts of long black hair.

Water poured from the sink faucets. The hairy blue creatures bobbed over the sink, gulping thirstily. Others hovered over the toilet, drinking their fill.

Evan gripped the doorknob so hard, his hand ached. He stared into the room, too horrified to move.

"The walls . . . ," he murmured in a trembling whisper. "Oh, no. The walls . . ."

The walls and ceiling and floor were covered with a layer of oozing blue slime. The pipe under the sink had been chewed clear through. Creatures bobbed beneath it, sucking up water. Others drank from puddles on the slime-covered floor.

"What are we going to —" Kermit started.

He didn't finish his sentence. A deafening *POP* rocked the little room as two Monster Blood creatures exploded to become four. A wave of cold, wet slime washed over Evan and Kermit.

Evan staggered back as several growling creatures bounced out of the bathroom. He saw three others pushing their way out through the basement window. Two were bouncing on the stairs.

"We've got to stop them!" he cried as another explosion and another flying wave of slime shook the room.

"But how?" Kermit whined.

Evan didn't have a chance to answer. A wet blue blob leaped onto his shoulder. With an angry snarl, it sank its teeth into Evan's sweatshirt.

Evan uttered a groan of pain. "It — it's sucking . . ." he stammered.

He ducked, swung around. And batted it away with a hard punch.

The creature roared furiously — and dove for Kermit.

Kermit dodged away — and fell over a hairy

blue blob. "Help me —!" he cried out as he landed on his back in a thick slime puddle. "They're totally fierce now!"

Kermit is right, Evan realized. There's nothing cute about these creatures now. They are ferocious — and deadly.

POP! POP!

And there are *more* of them every second!

Evan ducked away from another attacking creature. He reached both hands out and pulled Kermit to his feet.

"They're all getting away!" Evan declared.

"Maybe we should *let* them!" Kermit declared.

Evan glared at his cousin. "Do you want to be responsible for wrecking the whole town? OWWWW!" He cried out as a hairy blob bit into his ankle.

Evan kicked the creature away.

Kermit shook his head. "They drank up all my hair-growing formula. I'll never be able to mix it right again."

We were going to use it for my revenge against Conan, Evan thought bitterly. Well . . . forget that idea.

"We don't have time to worry about your hair formula," Evan told his cousin.

POP!

Another wave of slime slapped the bathroom wall.

"If they keep multiplying and multiplying,"

Evan said, "they could outnumber the people in this town. They could drink up the whole water supply. Drain all the flowers and plants. They could keep spreading and spreading — and drink up the entire country!"

Kermit gulped. "And it would be all my fault. I opened the can."

The growls and snarls and chomps of jagged teeth were deafening. Hairy blue creatures bounced out the window, up the steps, all around the basement.

"We have to get rid of them somehow," Evan moaned. "No. We can't just get rid of them. We have to *kill* them!"

"Oh, wow," Kermit muttered. Then his expression brightened. "I have an idea!" he declared.

21

"My electric fence!" he cried. "If we can herd them to the backyard, we can zap them with the electricity. Maybe it will dry them up!"

"Hey —!" Evan exclaimed. "Maybe it will. It's worth a try." Then he hesitated. "How do we get them to the backyard?"

Kermit shrugged.

POP! Another blob exploded into two.

Evan covered his ears to block out the angry growls and roars. He glanced frantically around the basement. And spotted several brooms and mops leaning against the wall near the laundry room.

"Come on — let's round them up!" he told Kermit.

He grabbed a broom and handed another one to his cousin. The two of them began swinging the brooms, batting the hairy blobs, poking them, moving them out.

The creatures squealed in protest. But their

balloonlike shape made them easy to bat and shove along.

It seemed to Evan to take hours. By the time they herded the last of the stragglers into the backyard, his arms ached and his sweatshirt was drenched with sweat.

"What's going on? What on earth are you doing?" Andy came running across the yard. She wore bright green leggings and a purple sweater. She goggled as she saw how many bouncing blobs the boys were herding.

"Yuck!" she groaned. "They're all hairy! Sick!"

"They're out of control!" Kermit declared. "And it's all my fault!"

Weird, Evan thought. Kermit never takes the blame for anything. Maybe he's growing up.

"That's why I came up with a brilliant plan to kill them!" Kermit declared.

Same old Kermit, Evan thought.

"We're going to zap them," Evan told Andy breathlessly. "On the invisible fence!"

"You're going to shock them to death?" she cried, staring at the bouncing, growling monsters.

"It's worth a try," Evan gasped. He slapped a blob into line with a swing of his broom. The black hair over its body stiffened and stood straight up. It tried to bite the broom handle. But Evan slapped it away with another swing.

"Get ready!" Kermit cried. He swung his broom

back and forth, frantically trying to keep the angry creatures in line.

"Okay! Push them! Push them forward — into the invisible fence!"

Evan swung his broom hard.

The blobs bounced forward, squealing and growling, snapping their teeth.

Forward. Forward. Toward the edge of the yard.

Will it work? Evan wondered. Will the jolt of electricity destroy the ugly, destructive things?

22

He swung the broom hard, batting the monsters forward.

Swung it again.

They bobbed and bounced over the low shrubs that divided the yards.

On into Conan Barber's backyard.

"Nooooooo!" Kermit let out a cry and slapped his forehead. "The switch! I forgot to turn it on again!"

Creatures bounced into the next yard. Beneath the tufts of black hair, their skin glowed bright blue in the morning sunlight.

"You jerk!" Evan shrieked at his cousin. "How could you forget again? How *could* you?"

Andy plopped down on the grass, lowering her head and uttering an unhappy sigh.

Kermit fumbled in his back pocket for the fence control. He finally tugged it out and pressed the red button to turn on the power.

ZZZAAAAAP!

Evan shrieked and leaped into the air as a powerful shock jolted through him.

"I *told* you not to stand there!" Kermit cried.

Evan jumped aside.

"I turned it up all the way!" Kermit declared.

"Too late," Evan muttered.

The Monster Blood creatures had all bounced and rolled into the next backyard.

Conan's yard.

"Oh, no," Evan moaned softly. "Here comes more trouble."

All three of them gasped as Conan came lumbering across his yard, a can of Coke in one hand, his other hand balled into a tight, angry fist.

23

"Conan — go back!" Evan warned. But his voice came out tiny and weak. He knew that Conan couldn't hear him over the growls and snarls of the Monster Blood creatures.

"What's the big idea?" Conan boomed. "It's not my birthday! Get these balloons out of my yard!"

"Get back! Get back!" Evan tried to warn him.

Kermit and Andy stood frozen, watching Conan storm toward the bouncing, evil blobs.

Evan waved frantically with both hands. "Get back —!"

Conan scowled at him. "Are you ordering me around in my own yard?"

"But — but —" Evan sputtered.

Conan kicked at one of the creatures. "Whoa. This balloon has hair on it!"

He bent to pick the creature up — and it jumped onto his arm. With a growl, it swallowed Conan's Coke can.

"Hey —!" Conan protested.

The creature started to swell up from the liquid.

Conan struggled to shake it off. But it clung tightly to his arm.

And then, with a loud, wet *POP*, it exploded.

Thick slime splashed over Conan's face. He spluttered, thrashed his arms out in surprise. Wiped the slimy goo from his eyes.

And blinked at *two* hairy, round creatures clinging to his arm.

"Get these *off* me!" he shrieked.

With a furious cry, he swung his free arm — and batted the two blobs together. They made a loud *SQUISH* as they collided with each other. And they dropped to the ground.

Another creature bit into Conan's leg. Conan stumbled and tripped over another one.

He pulled himself up quickly, glaring furiously at Kermit. "You invented these hairy things — didn't you!" he accused. "Don't even answer. It's some kind of lab experiment — right? I know this is your kind of thing."

"No. Listen —" Kermit started weakly.

Another Monster Blood creature exploded, sending a wave of cold slime over Conan.

He spluttered again and tried to wipe it away. Then he shook a fist at them. "It'll be payback time — real soon," he threatened. "Payback time!"

And he slunk back toward his house, covered in slime.

Evan breathed a sigh of relief. We have enough problems without having Conan in our face, he thought.

Of course, Conan will be back. But we can't worry about that now.

He gazed over the backyards. The Monster Blood creatures were spreading out over the entire block.

What are we going to do? Evan wondered.

He turned back to the house. "Hey — Aunt Dee is home!" he cried.

"When did she get back?" Kermit wondered.

"We have to tell her what's happened," Andy urged. "We need help. We can't round these creatures up on our own."

The three of them took off, running across the slime-puddled grass to the back door. A few seconds later, they burst breathlessly into the kitchen.

Kermit's mom had her back to them. She was stirring a long spoon in a big aluminum pot on the stove. She turned as the storm door slammed.

"What's up, guys?" She smiled at them.

"We need help!" Kermit blurted out.

Aunt Dee's smile faded. "Help? What's wrong?" She turned back to the stove. "Keep talking. I just have to stir this. I'm mixing up a new batch of spaghetti with hot sauce for my reading club tonight."

"We have a real problem. Andy found a can of Monster Blood, and Kermit opened it," Evan told her, all in one breath.

"That's nice," Aunt Dee replied, frowning at her hot sauce. She sniffed and peered down into the steaming pot. "I think it needs more peppers."

"Mom — you've got to *listen*!" Kermit pleaded.

"I am listening," she insisted, stirring harder. "Go on with your story."

"It's not a story. It's real," Evan told her.

Still stirring, she glanced back at him. "I hope there isn't any serious trouble, Evan. You are in charge, you know. Being out in the middle of the night and ruining my flower garden is enough trouble for one visit. When I tell your parents —"

"Mom, *please*!" Kermit begged.

"I'm afraid we *do* have more trouble," Andy told her.

"The Monster Blood poured out and formed a little blob creature," Evan continued, his voice trembling. "It was cute at first. But it drank a lot of water and exploded into two. Then the two exploded into four."

Evan glanced out the kitchen window. The creatures were rolling and bouncing all over the backyard. Some of them had discovered the garden hose and were soaking up water, inflating rapidly.

Several of them were forcing their way into the big wooden doghouse in a corner of the yard.

Oh, no, Evan thought. That's where I stashed the Super-Soakers. Plenty of water for them in Dogface's house.

"Now there are hundreds of them, Mom," Kermit continued the story. "And they're not cute anymore. They've grown hair, and they've turned really fierce. They're spreading out all over the neighborhood, and —"

"That's nice," Aunt Dee said absently, frowning at her hot sauce.

"Mom — just take a look at them!" Kermit pleaded. "Look out the window. Now!"

"I can't right now," she replied. "I have to stir —"

The phone rang.

She handed the long wooden spoon to Evan. "I've been waiting for that call. Stir for me till I get back, okay?"

Before Evan could reply, she ran from the kitchen.

"I don't think she heard us," Kermit said, shaking his head unhappily. "If only she would take one look out the window. Then maybe . . ." His voice drifted off.

Evan sighed and stirred the sauce. The steam rising up from the pot burned his eyes. "This stuff is deadly!" he declared.

And that gave him an idea.

He glanced out the window in time to see a wet explosion of slime from the doghouse. The creatures had found the Super-Soakers. More of them had clustered around the little wooden structure.

He turned to Kermit and Andy. "Let's try Aunt Dee's hot sauce," he whispered.

"Excuse me?" Kermit and Andy stared at him, confused.

"You want to eat now?" Kermit asked. "I thought you hated Mom's hot sauce."

"I do," Evan admitted, still whispering. "Because it *kills*!"

"I get it!" Andy declared, her dark eyes widening in excitement. "You think maybe the hot sauce will kill the Monster Blood creatures."

Evan nodded. "It's liquid. So they'll try to drink it. And maybe it will be too hot for them to handle."

"Maybe it will blow them up for good!" Andy exclaimed.

"Worth a try, I guess," Kermit said softly.

Evan glanced to the door. No sign of Aunt Dee.

"Quick —" he whispered. "Help me carry the pot outside."

24

Evan grabbed two pot holders off the counter and handed one to Andy. Then they each grabbed a handle on the top of the big stew pot and lifted it carefully off the stove.

"It weighs a ton," Andy groaned.

"Mom likes to make a lot of hot sauce," Kermit explained. "She keeps the extra sauce in the freezer. For emergencies, I guess."

He held the back door open. Evan and Andy, hoisting the steaming pot between them, carried it out the door.

Evan raised his eyes to the backyard and let out a cry. "We may be too late," he moaned. "There are so many of them!"

Squinting into the sunlight, he thought he saw *thousands* of them! They bounced and rolled over backyards. They growled and grunted.

They gulped water from the garden hose. Dozens of them were bouncing through a neighbor's flower bed, drinking the plants dry.

Two houses down, Monster Blood creatures had gathered in a small, backyard goldfish pond. They were busily drinking the pond dry. Some of them were sucking the liquid out of the goldfish!

"Too late," Evan murmured. "We're just too late."

"It might work," Andy said, not very enthusiastically. "If we can get them to drink it."

"I — I have to set it down," Evan told her. "The handle is hot. My hand is burning."

"Mine too," Andy replied.

They set the steaming stew pot down on the grass in the center of the yard.

"Now how do we get them to try it?" Kermit asked. Without waiting for an answer, he cupped his hands around his mouth and began shouting, "Come and get it! Come and get it!"

Evan grabbed him and pulled him back. "I don't think they speak English," he told Kermit, rolling his eyes.

"Let's back away from the pot and let them discover it on their own," Andy suggested.

"Good idea," Evan replied. He tugged Kermit back some more. "They haven't had any trouble finding liquid everywhere. If we step back a bit, they'll discover the hot sauce."

The three of them backed toward the garage, keeping their eyes on the pot of hot sauce.

Monster Blood creatures bounced over three or

four backyards, sucking up any liquid they could find. Flower beds lay wilted and dead. Large patches of grass were brown and dry.

Will they find the hot sauce? Evan wondered.

Will they try it? Will it destroy them?

It nearly destroyed me! he remembered. It burned my lips and took all the skin off the roof of my mouth!

Will it burn up the hairy blue blobs?

The spicy aroma of the hot sauce drifted to Evan's nose. You can probably smell it all over the backyards, he guessed.

He stared without blinking at the aluminum pot gleaming in the sunlight. And he crossed his fingers, hoping his idea would work.

As he watched, a few Monster Blood creatures turned toward the pot. Their round eyes bulged. They began bobbing up and down, as if excited.

Then they started to bounce toward the hot sauce.

"Yesssss!" Evan whispered. "Yessss!"

But before the creatures could reach the pot, another figure came bounding into the backyard.

Evan was concentrating so hard, at first he didn't recognize the big sheepdog. But Kermit's cries made Evan realize what was happening.

"Dogface — get away!" Kermit cried frantically. "Dogface — no! Go home, boy! Dogface — go home!"

But the big dog ignored Kermit's cries. Wagging his stub of a tail furiously, he trotted toward the shining hot sauce pot.

25

"Dogface — get away!" Kermit cried, frantically waving the big sheepdog back.

Panting hard, his pink tongue hanging down from his furry face, Dogface bounded up to the hot sauce pot. Ignoring Kermit's desperate cries, he lowered his head to the pot and sniffed it.

"No! Go away! Go away!" Evan joined in on Kermit's cries. "Get him away from there!"

They couldn't move fast enough.

The big dog bumped the pot over. The orange hot sauce poured out over the grass.

Dogface lowered his head and licked up a few tastes.

Blue Monster Blood creatures bounced closer. A few began hungrily drinking up the spilled hot sauce.

Evan waited and watched, his fingers crossed so hard, they hurt.

No. No.

The hot sauce didn't bother the hairy blue blobs a bit.

But Dogface raised his head from the ground. Behind his thick fur, his black eyes rolled crazily. The big dog opened his jaws in a long howl of pain.

And as he howled, a growling blue blob leaped onto the dog's back.

Stunned and in pain, Dogface shook himself hard. But the creature clung to the fur on his back.

"No! Get away!" Evan shrieked as another blob leaped onto Kermit's dog.

With another howl, the big dog took off. His big paws pounded the grass. He shook himself as he ran, trying to throw off the two creatures.

Kermit stood openmouthed in shock.

"The blobs are drinking up all the hot sauce!" Andy declared. "And now they're biting and snapping at each other! It's turning them even meaner!"

"Come on!" Evan cried, running after the dog. "We've got to save Dogface! Those creatures will kill him!"

Evan took a deep breath and started running full speed, following the howling dog. Kermit and Andy ran right behind him.

"Dogface — whoa!" Kermit called. "Dogface — stop! Stop!"

But, as always, the dog ignored Kermit.

Shaking his back, he ran in crazy zigzags.

Through backyards. And then across a street. And onto the sidewalk.

The dog barked and howled in protest. But the two blobs hung on, appearing to enjoy the ride.

"Dogface — wait!" Kermit pleaded.

The three kids ran as fast as they could, zigzagging across streets and yards, following the barking, frightened dog.

As they neared the school, Evan glanced back. And saw that the Monster Blood creatures were following them. Dozens of them, bouncing and rolling over the front yards.

They were growling and snapping at everything in their path. One of them exploded, sending a spray of slime over someone's front yard.

"They're all following us!" Evan cried breathlessly.

Kermit and Andy turned back. "Oh, wow!" Kermit muttered. "It's like a *parade*!"

"Hey — what's *that*?" Evan heard a woman shout. "What are you kids doing?"

"Hey — get off my grass!" He heard a man's angry cry.

He heard startled voices. And saw people bursting out of their houses. Two kids jumped off their bikes and stared. A man on a ladder cried out in surprise and nearly toppled to the ground.

"Dogface — please *stop*!" Kermit wailed.

But the big dog galloped across the street, heading to the playground behind the school. Just past the sidewalk, he stopped and began rubbing his back against a wide tree trunk.

The hairy blobs on the dog's back bounced and scraped against the rough tree bark. But they held on tight.

With another howl, Dogface took off, running wildly across the softball field, kicking up dust in the infield, bucking his head, shaking his whole body.

And then the big dog slumped to the ground.

The three kids gasped as Dogface toppled onto his side.

The two blobs had their mouths buried in the dog's thick fur.

Dogface kicked out once with all four legs.

And then didn't move.

26

"They killed him! They *killed* him!" Kermit screamed.

"No!" Evan cried. "He's still breathing!"

Sprawled on his side, the big dog's chest heaved. The ugly creatures gulped hard, bobbing on top of the dog's thick fur.

Evan and Andy dove for the dog. Evan grabbed one of the drinking creatures in both hands. He twisted it hard — then tugged it off.

The blob opened its wet mouth in an angry roar. It snapped its blue jaws at Evan.

Evan raised it up and heaved it into the sea of bobbing blue creatures that swarmed over the playground.

Then he turned to Andy. She struggled to pull off the remaining blob.

She gave a hard pull. "Yuck! This hair is so gross!" she wailed. Her hands slid off, and she stumbled back.

Dogface uttered a weak groan. The dog's big eyes rolled crazily in his head.

Evan grabbed the hairy blob. He twisted it hard, the way he twisted the first one. He pulled up with all his strength.

The creature lifted off Dogface with a loud *POP*. It snarled furiously and snapped its jaws over Evan's wrist.

"OWWW!" Evan howled in pain.

He turned and heaved the ugly creature as high and far as he could. It bounced off a tree limb, then fell into the crowd of bobbing Monster Blood creatures.

Dogface climbed quickly to his feet. He shook himself hard. He seemed to be okay.

Kermit squatted down to hug him.

Evan gazed over the playground. Monster Blood creatures swarmed over the softball field, over the volleyball courts, over the whole block!

People came out of houses and came running to the playground. Evan heard the wail of a siren — and saw a black-and-white police cruiser turn the corner. It squealed to a halt, and two dark-uniformed officers came scrambling out.

Andy bumped up against Evan. "Bad news," she said, frowning. "I don't think we can keep this a secret anymore."

Evan shook his head. He knew Andy was making a joke. But this was no time to be funny.

He had been in trouble before. He had the whole town chasing him last year, when Monster Blood had turned him into a giant.

And now, Monster Blood had gotten him in major trouble once again. How could he ever explain this? What could the police do against these horrible, frightening creatures?

POP! A fat blob exploded into two.

Across the playground, people pushed closer to get a better view.

The creatures were roaring now, roaring like angry tigers. They bit at each other and chewed the ground.

The two police officers were struggling to force their way through the angry, bouncing creatures. One of the officers had a phone to his ear. Probably calling for more officers, Evan thought.

Behind him, he heard a weak cry.

Evan spun around — and gasped. Hairy blobs had leaped onto Kermit. One sat on top of Kermit's blond hair. Two more had climbed to his shoulders. Another perched on his back.

"Help . . . ," Kermit choked out. He thrashed his arms and tried to squirm out from under the creatures.

But they spread out over him, digging their mouths into his skin.

"Ohhhh." Kermit uttered a groan and fell to his knees.

And several more creatures leaped onto him. They made wet sucking noises as they covered his body. Kermit disappeared beneath them.

"YAAAIIII!"

Evan heard another shrill cry. He turned to see Andy covered in hairy creatures too. She swung her fists furiously, trying to bat them away.

She ducked and squirmed and shook herself.

But they spread over her shoulders, down her arms. One of them leaped up and grabbed on to her hair. It spread itself wetly over her face.

Evan dove for Kermit. He slipped and landed hard on his knees. He grabbed at a blob on Kermit's shoulder and tugged it.

It came off with a wet *POP.*

Evan grabbed for another one.

But before he could pull it off, he felt a cold, wet slap on the back of his neck.

Then he felt a heavy, wet blob thump onto his head. Cold slime ran down Evan's face.

He reached up. Tried to grab the evil thing.

Too late.

Two more blobs leaped onto him and attached themselves to his back.

"Can't . . . breathe. . . ," Evan gasped.

The weight of the creatures pushed him down. Down . . .

Facedown in the wet grass.

He dug his elbows into the ground. Tried to push up. Tried to struggle to his knees.

I've got to get up, he told himself. *I can't let them cover me like a blanket.*

Like a smothering blanket . . .

But the creatures were too heavy. There were too many of them on him.

He let out a whimper of pain as he felt mouths biting at him. Drinking . . .

Choking off his air. Smothering him . . .

I'm doomed, Evan realized.

This time, the Monster Blood got me. This time, the Monster Blood wins.

27

The creatures covered Evan. Darkness swept over him.

He struggled to breathe.

He wondered if Kermit and Andy were being smothered beside him.

He sucked in a mouthful of air. A cold, wet blob pressed over his face. Evan couldn't let the air out.

He heard a rush, a buzz in his ears.

The sound of my own blood, he thought. My own blood pulsing through my veins.

He suddenly felt lighter.

I'm fading, he thought.

He let out the mouthful of air.

Hey — the creature moved away from my face! Evan realized.

What's going on?

He raised his head — and saw an amazing sight.

Kermit and Andy were climbing to their feet. The blobs had moved away from them. They had moved away — to fight the other blobs.

They're all fighting each other! Evan saw.

Furious growls rose over the playground as the creatures bit each other, tugged at hair, at slimy blue flesh, dug their pointy teeth into each other.

With a groan, Evan climbed to his knees. He shook off his dizziness and gazed at the incredible scene.

"They're *swallowing* each other!" Andy gasped. "They turned so mean, they're going after *each other*!"

She's right, Evan realized. They're getting meaner and meaner. So mean, they're destroying each other!

Kermit picked up his glasses from the ground. He wiped off some blades of grass, then slid them over his face. "I don't believe it!" he cried, watching the creatures devour each other.

In minutes, the blobs had eaten each other. They had completely vanished.

The grass was covered with slime and wet tufts of black hair.

The last blob left rolled over and died, its blue flesh ripped to shreds. But nothing else remained of the hundreds of creatures.

Not a trace.

Evan stood up shakily. He dusted himself off. Squinting into the sunlight, he looked around.

Groups of neighborhood people talked excitedly. They shook their heads and shrugged their shoulders as they talked, trying to make sense of the whole thing.

I could make sense of it for them, Evan thought. But they'd never believe me.

He turned to Kermit and Andy. "Are you okay?"

They nodded. Andy pulled a chunk of slime from her dark hair.

"Let's get out of here," Kermit said.

But before Evan could move, a shadow fell over him.

He turned and stared up at the two grim-faced police officers. "You again," one of them accused, narrowing his dark eyes at Evan.

"I . . . I . . . ," Evan stammered.

"I think you three kids are in big trouble," the other officer said softly.

"Trouble?" Evan choked out. "Why? What did we do?"

The officers gazed around the playground.

"What did we do?" Kermit repeated shrilly. "We didn't do anything wrong. We didn't commit any crime."

"There's nothing here," Andy added. "Look around. There's nothing here to blame us for."

"Well . . ." The officers hesitated.

One of them picked up a slimy wad of black hair from the grass. "How about littering?" he asked his partner. "I think we can charge them with littering."

"Let's forget about it," the other officer muttered. He turned to the three kids. "Go on. Go home. Let's forget any of this ever happened."

I hope I can, Evan thought as he turned and started jogging away with the others.

I hope I can forget about it.

"That was a close one," Kermit said softly as they jogged across the street.

"Yeah. A close one," Andy repeated.

"I just feel bad I never got to look at one of those guys under a microscope," Kermit said.

"Yuck," Andy murmured. Her whole body shivered. "I keep thinking about that disgusting hair on their bodies. It felt so wet and slimy when it brushed against your skin."

"What a waste of good hair-growing formula!" Kermit grumbled.

"Let's stop talking about it," Evan suggested. "That policeman is right. We should try to forget the whole thing."

They didn't say a word for the rest of the way back. Evan started to feel better as Kermit's house came into view.

Maybe this horrible adventure is over, he told himself.

But his heart sank, and a heavy feeling of dread swept over him when he saw Aunt Dee waiting for them on the front stoop.

"Evan, you are responsible," she said sternly,

narrowing her eyes angrily at him. "I want a full explanation."

"Well . . ." Evan didn't know where to begin.

"I shouldn't have opened the can of Monster Blood," Kermit told her.

"That's what started it," Evan said. "Then the blue creatures started exploding, and —"

"Stop right now!" Aunt Dee ordered, raising her hand in a halt sign. "I don't want to hear about your silly blue creatures. If you want to waste your time on fantasy games, that's your business."

She crossed her arms in front of her and glared at Evan angrily. "I want to know what happened to my pot of hot sauce!"

"Huh?" Evan gasped.

The whole town was nearly overrun by gross, water-sucking monsters. And all she cares about is her precious hot sauce!

"I'm waiting," Aunt Dee said sternly, tapping her foot.

"Well . . . ," Evan started.

What can I tell her? he asked himself, thinking hard. What can I say?

"Evan took your hot sauce," Kermit chimed in. "He ate it, Mom. Evan loves your hot sauce. He ate the whole pot himself."

I don't believe this! Evan groaned to himself. After all we've been through, the little rat just got me in trouble again!

111

But to Evan's surprise, he found Aunt Dee smiling at him. "Evan, I'm so flattered," she said. "I didn't know you liked it so much. I'll make you a big pot of it *every time* you come for a visit!"

"Uh . . . great," Evan replied weakly.

"Go get my stew pot. Then come inside for lunch," she instructed them. She disappeared into the house.

Evan led the way around to the back. He scowled at Kermit. "I can't believe you told your mom that."

Kermit shrugged. "It was the only thing I could think of."

Evan gazed around the backyard. The flower garden was dead and dry. Big patches of grass lay brown and flat.

The stew pot sat on its side in the middle of the yard.

Evan started toward it — but stopped with a startled cry as a figure staggered out from behind the garage.

A hulking creature with glowing red eyes!

28

"Whoa!" Evan exclaimed.

Kermit and Andy huddled close to him as the creature lumbered into view.

As it stepped into the bright sunlight, Evan saw that it wasn't a creature at all. The three of them were staring at a man in a white work suit.

The work suit looked like the kind of space suit worn by astronauts. It covered the man from head to foot. The man's face was completely covered too. He peered out at them through bright red goggles.

"Who — who *are* you?" Evan managed to choke out.

The man stopped halfway across the yard. He stared out at them, his eyes dark behind the red goggles. Finally, he lifted a gloved hand and pulled back his hood.

He removed the goggles, took a few deep breaths, and pushed his curly black hair off his forehead. "No blue creatures here?" he asked, looking around. "I guess I didn't need the safety suit."

"Who — who are you?" Evan stammered again.

"I'm looking for my little blue guys," the man replied. "I heard there was quite a fuss at the playground. The police said you might be able to help me."

"Those are *your* creatures?" Andy cried.

The man nodded. "Allow me to introduce myself. I'm Professor Eric Crane. From the Science Institute downtown." He glanced once again around the yard. "Do you have the can?"

"I — I kept it in the garage," Evan told him. "But how do we know it's yours? Who are you? Why are you wearing that uniform?"

"Did you really invent those disgusting blue blobs?" Andy demanded.

The man took a few steps toward them. The safety uniform was so big and bulky, he walked awkwardly and slowly.

"Bring me the can, and I'll explain," he told them.

Evan obediently brought the plastic can from the garage. He put it into Professor Crane's gloved hand.

"Those creatures — they got meaner and meaner," Andy told him. "They got so mean, they ate each other up."

The professor sighed. "I know," he said. "That's

why I threw them away. My underwater fighting force was a total failure."

"Excuse me?" Evan cried. "Fighting force?"

"I developed the blue liquid in my lab," Professor Crane explained. "It was supposed to be a monster fighting force. For underwater combat. A special army of fighters who would get meaner and meaner, and multiply underwater until they outnumbered the enemy."

"Cool idea," Kermit murmured. And then he added, "I guess."

Professor Crane shrugged. "But it didn't work. They get too mean. It was a bad experiment."

He glanced down at the can in his gloved hand. "But I should have been more careful when I tossed the can out. Much more careful." The professor shook his head. "I spent ten years on this. Ten years and fifty million dollars. All a waste. All a total waste."

With a bitter sigh, he started to pull the lid off the can.

But he let out a startled cry as Dogface bumped him from behind. The big sheepdog ran hard into Professor Crane — and the Monster Blood can flew out of his hand.

Evan watched it bounce over a low shrub and roll to a stop in Conan's yard.

"That's okay," Evan told him. "It's empty."

Professor Crane shrugged and uttered another

unhappy sigh. "Ten years . . .," he murmured. "Ten years . . ."

Shaking his head, he stomped off. He turned back to them when he reached the driveway. "You won't tell anyone about this, will you?" he called. "It would be very embarrassing to me if you did."

"No problem," Evan replied.

He watched the scientist lumber down the drive. Then Evan turned back to Kermit and Andy.

For some reason, Kermit was giggling.

"What's so funny?" Evan asked.

Kermit pointed. "Look. Conan came running out. He discovered the Monster Blood can."

"But it's empty — isn't it?" Evan cried. "Isn't it?"

He started to run toward Conan. But Kermit held him back.

"Kermit — let me go!" Evan demanded. "We have to warn Conan. That stuff is dangerous. If there is any of it left in there, and he opens it —"

"I think there's a tiny bit left in the can," Kermit told Evan. "You wanted your revenge — didn't you? This is perfect. Conan will let the stuff out, and in a few minutes he'll have bouncing blue blobs to take care of."

"But — but —" Evan sputtered.

"It'll be funny," Andy agreed. "Conan will be terrified. He won't know what to do with them. They'll suck up his whole yard. It's a great re-

116

venge, Evan. And it's harmless. They'll just eat each other in the end."

"Meanwhile, Conan will have the most frightening time of his life," Kermit added gleefully.

"Okay, okay," Evan agreed. "You're right. It's pretty funny. Let's not warn him."

"Lunchtime! Come on in, you guys!" Aunt Dee called from the kitchen door.

Evan glanced back as he followed the others into the house. Conan had the blue can in his hands. He popped open the lid.

Evan giggled to himself and went in to lunch.

After lunch, they carried the dishes into the kitchen and loaded them in the dishwasher. "What do you want to do this afternoon?" Kermit asked. "How about some experiments in my lab?"

"No way!" Andy replied.

Evan heard Conan calling them. "Hey, you three! Hey, guys!" Conan shouted from the backyard.

Evan led the way out the door. He couldn't keep a smile from spreading across his face. Conan probably wants us to help him round up the blue blobs, he thought.

But to his surprise, he saw no blue blobs in the backyard.

"What's going on?" Evan asked Conan.

Conan grinned at him. "I found that blue candy of yours," he said.

"Huh? Blue candy?" Evan gasped.

Conan nodded. "Yeah. You remember. That candy you wouldn't share with me the other night. I found it and I ate it. It was pretty good. Sticky, but good."

"But — but —" Evan sputtered.

"Now I just have two small problems," Conan continued. "For one thing, I can't stop drinking water."

"What's the other problem?" Evan asked in a trembling voice.

"Look," Conan replied. He waved toward his backyard.

And a figure came running out from the house. Another Conan!

That Conan was followed by two more Conans!

The four Conans swept around Evan, Kermit, and Andy, and formed a circle around them.

"*This* is my other problem," Conan said, narrowing his eyes menacingly at Evan. "There are four of us now. And I don't know why — but we're feeling MEANER than usual!"

About R.L. Stine

R.L. Stine is the most popular author in America. He is the creator of the *Goosebumps, Give Yourself Goosebumps, Fear Street*, and *Ghosts of Fear Street* series, among other popular books. He has written more than 100 scary novels for kids. Bob lives in New York City with his wife, Jane, teenage son, Matt, and dog, Nadine.